W9-BUF-680

For Lucy,
Sophie,
and
Brendan

Hazel and Twig
THE BIRTHDAY FORTUNE

Brenna Burns Yu

CANDLEWICK PRESS

HAZEL'S little sister, Twig, was much smaller than Hazel. She followed Hazel everywhere.

Hazel could fly her kite higher than the Queen Anne's lace. Twig was happy to chase the string.

Twig didn't know weeds from flowers. Hazel knew violets from buttercups. "Let's pick some for Umma," Hazel said.

"They're beautiful!" their mother said, and she put the weeds and the flowers into a vase together.

"What are you working on?" Hazel asked.
"I'm writing invitations!" said Umma.
It was almost Twig's first birthday!

Hazel sealed the envelopes.
Twig liked to help, too.

While they waited for the mail snail to collect the invitations, Hazel told Twig how they would tell her fortune at the party. "It's called a doljabi! We'll put out lots of things, like a lute and a ball of yarn and some toasted thistle seeds. Then you'll go pick one — only one, OK? If you pick the lute it means you'll be a musician, and the yarn means you'll have a really long life."

The seeds meant peace and plenty. There would be a book for a scholar, a hammer for a builder, a brush for an artist, and a stethoscope for a doctor, too.

Hazel said, “Uh-oh! If you pick the brush it will be very messy around here.”

They spent days getting ready.

Appa and Hazel made dandelion kimchi and fiddlehead soup. Twig banged pots with a spoon.

Halmoni arrived with clover kimchi, rainbow rice cakes, and a kiss for each granddaughter.

"What did I choose at my doljabi?" Hazel asked, even though she knew the answer.

"The yarn," Halmoni said. Hazel loved that. She wanted to live to be twice as old as Halmoni, at least!

“What will Twig choose?” Hazel asked.

“We’ll have to wait and see,” said Appa.

“I hope she picks the yarn,” said Hazel, “so we can live a long time together.”

The night before the party, Appa gathered fireflies for the lanterns. Umma hung out the beautiful hanboks that Hazel and Twig would get to wear.

Twig yawned. She didn't know it would be her birthday in the morning. She just wanted to tug on the long sash of her hanbok.

Hazel was too excited to sleep. She could not wait to put on her hanbok the next day. She could not wait to see what Twig would choose.

When the sun came up over the tall oak, the guests arrived.

"Happy birthday!" Grandma Thistle said, tying a balloon around Twig's wrist.

"Hazel! Twig! You're growing like milkweeds," Grandpa Thistle said.

Before long, the party was hopping.

Everyone was wondering what Twig would choose at the doljabi.

But Twig was too busy watching her balloon float away to pay any attention to all that.

Soon it was time for the doljabi! Umma and Appa unrolled a carpet and laid out the objects. Hazel held her breath and crossed her fingers. Twig reached out her paw and started to walk.

Then she stopped.
She looked up.

Hazel looked up.
Everyone looked up.

Twig reached up as the feather floated down. It landed in her paw.

This had never happened before. What could it mean?

Appa scratched his head. "A feather means . . . she'll be very ticklish?"

"No, Appa!" Hazel was disappointed. Then she thought about Twig. "Twig likes my kite. She let her balloon fly away. . . . A feather means Twig will fly someday!"

Everyone oohed and aahed and clapped tiny paws.

So the party buzzed along, full of happy mouse-chatter.
It turned out that Grandpa Thistle was the very ticklish one.

They nibbled cake until the fireflies set the lanterns aglow.

“But I wonder,” Hazel murmured sleepily, “could a mouse really fly?”

H
T

They would all just have to wait and see.

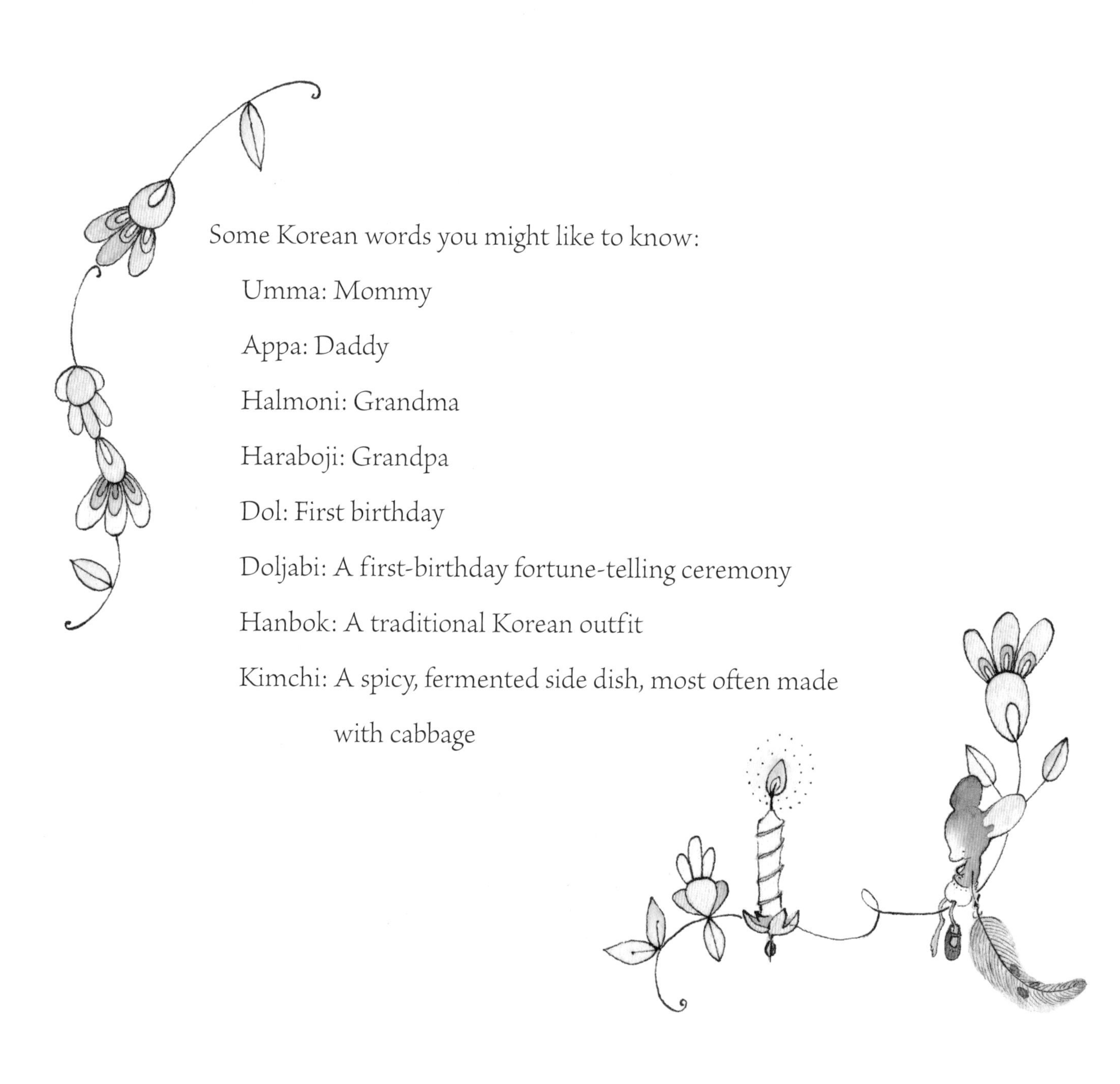

Some Korean words you might like to know:

Umma: Mommy

Appa: Daddy

Halmoni: Grandma

Haraboji: Grandpa

Dol: First birthday

Doljabi: A first-birthday fortune-telling ceremony

Hanbok: A traditional Korean outfit

Kimchi: A spicy, fermented side dish, most often made with cabbage

When a Korean or Korean-American mouse (or human!) turns one, the family throws a big celebration. For a woodland mouse, this feast usually takes place at the foot of a tree. There is lots of special food: barbecued acorns, fiddlehead soup, wildflower bibimbap, dandelion kimchi, and more. (Humans generally celebrate at home or in a banquet hall, and they prefer barbecued meats and vegetables, seafood pancakes, steamed rice, dumpling soup, and spicy cabbage kimchi.) Mouse or human, the baby wears a traditional Korean outfit called a hanbok. A dolsang, or dol table, is piled high with fruits and other symbols of health and good luck. The highlight of the party is the doljabi ceremony, when the baby chooses an object from a collection of meaningful items. Usually there are traditional objects, like yarn and a book, along with some modern choices, like a stethoscope and a microphone. The family might also include items with special meaning for them. Whatever the baby chooses is said to predict its future!

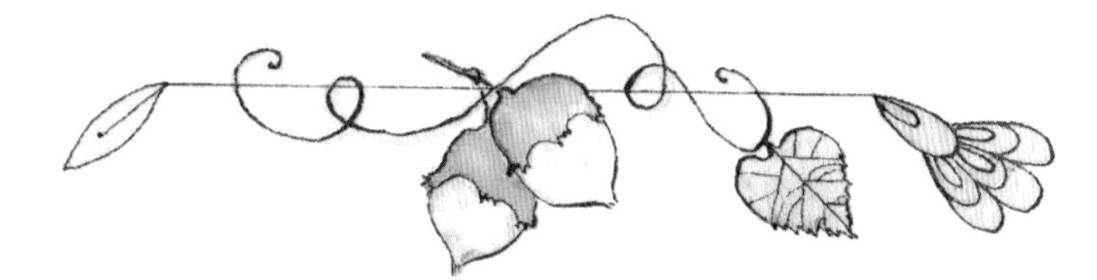

Thank you to everyone who guided me on the romanization of Korean words and helped to make sure the story was culturally accurate, especially Annie Koh, Sang Pahk, Hee Young, and Yoni.

First edition 2018

Library of Congress Catalog Card Number pending
ISBN 978-0-7636-8970-4

18 19 20 21 22 23 CCP 10 9 8 7 6 5 4 3 2 1

Printed in Shenzhen, Guangdong, China

This book was typeset in Brioso Pro.
The illustrations were done in ink and watercolor.

Candlewick Press
99 Dover Street
Somerville, Massachusetts 02144

visit us at www.candlewick.com